I'm Reading About

YELLOWSTONE

National Park

GALLOPADE

by Carole Marsh

Printed and Manufactured in Peachtree City, GA., USA www.gallopade.com

Book design: Susan Van Denhende

Editor: Janice Baker

Yellowstone National Park
is a great place to visit!

What is so special about
Yellowstone National Park?

Let's read about it and see!

NATIONAL PARK

What is a national park?

A national park is a large area of land
set aside by a country.
The land is kept natural and pure.
Animals roam free.

National parks are fun for
people to visit and enjoy!

Park Entrance

PARK RANGERS

I am a park ranger!

I work at Yellowstone National Park.
My job is to protect the park.
I make sure people do not harm
the land, plants, or animals.

I am an expert on Yellowstone National Park.
You can ask me lots of questions!

Park Ranger

LOCATION

Yellowstone National Park is located in three states.
Most of the park is in Wyoming.
Parts of the park are in Montana and Idaho.

Yellowstone is a very big park!

The United States has
59 national parks.

Yellowstone National Park

HISTORY

Yellowstone National Park became a park in 1872.
It was the first national park in America!

Isn't it grand
that America took a stand
to protect our land!

President Ulysses S. Grant signed the law that created Yellowstone National Park.

First National Park

VOLCANO

Yellowstone National Park has a little secret.
Actually, it has a BIG secret!
The park sits on top of a huge volcano!
The volcano is so big it is known as a "supervolcano."

A volcano is an opening in the Earth's crust.
When a volcano erupts, hot gases, lava,
and ashes burst out!

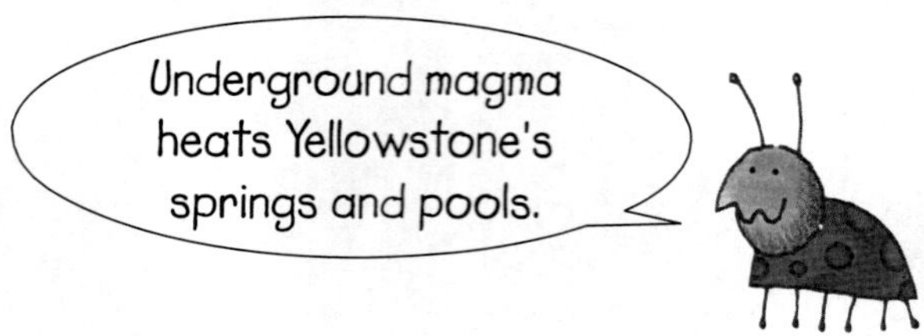

Grand Prismatic Spring

GEYSERS & SPRINGS

Many sights at Yellowstone let you know
there is a volcano under your feet.

Giant geysers shoot hot water
high into the sky!
Hot springs steam and bubble!
Mud pots gurgle and boil!

Hot Springs

OLD FAITHFUL

I am a famous geyser at Yellowstone.
My name is "Old Faithful."
I got my name because I erupt on a regular basis.
I erupt about 17 times each day!

Old Faithful's steam shoots up more than 100 feet in the air!

Old Faithful Geyser

Yellowstone Lake

LAKE

I am Yellowstone Lake!
I am the largest lake in Yellowstone National Park.
Motorboats, sailboats, canoes, and kayaks glide across me.

Yellowstone Lake freezes over for half the year!

Grand Canyon of the Yellowstone

Have you ever seen a waterfall?
Have you ever seen a canyon?
Yellowstone has them both—
in the "Grand Canyon of the Yellowstone"!

The Yellowstone River
carved this beautiful canyon.
The canyon walls are red,
yellow, white, and pink!

CANYON

Bison

I am a bison!
I live in Yellowstone National Park.
Some people call me a buffalo.
Either way, call me BIG!

I am the largest land mammal in North America.
I can weigh up to 2,000 pounds.

Even though I am big, I can run fast.
So watch out!

ANIMALS

Black Bears

I am a black bear!
I live in Yellowstone National Park.
Grizzly bears live here too.

Bears hibernate.
We eat a lot in summer and fall.
Then, we live off our fat
while we sleep through winter!

Yellowstone Animals

ANIMALS

There are many more animals
in Yellowstone National Park!

There are tall ones like elk and moose.
There are fast ones like coyotes and cougars.
There are water-loving ones like beavers and otters.
There are small ones like pikas and gophers.

Outdoor Fun

THINGS TO DO

There many things to do
at Yellowstone National Park!

Hike **Ride Bikes** **Ride Horses** **Camp** **Take Pictures** **Birdwatch**

Whatever you choose,
you will have fun!
Yellowstone has activities
for everyone!

Winter Fun

THINGS TO DO

Winter in Yellowstone
means only one thing:
put on your mittens
and play in the snow 'til spring!

Ski

Snowshoe

Snowmobile

Snow Play!

Water Fun

If you like the water,
Yellowstone's the place for you!

You can ride in a boat
to see the sights.
Or grab a pole
and fish until night!

Canoe **Kayak** **Scenic Cruise** **Fish**

THINGS TO DO

Old Faithful Inn

DID YOU KNOW?

Read these world-famous facts about Yellowstone!

Yellowstone National Park has:

- The world's largest group of geysers
- The world's largest herd of free-roaming bison
- The world's largest log cabin building: Old Faithful Inn

GLOSSARY

bison: a large animal of the cow family with a shaggy mane and short curved horns

canyon: a deep valley with steep rock sides that usually has a river running through it

erupt: to burst out in a sudden explosion

geyser: a natural hot spring that shoots out hot water and steam

hibernate: to spend the winter in a sleeping, inactive state

mammal: a warm-blooded animal that feeds milk to its young and has hair or fur

pika: a small mammal related to rabbits with short, rounded ears and short legs

volcano: an opening in the Earth's crust through which lava, ash, and hot gases flow